JUSTICE LEAGUE™

RACE TO SAVE THE DAY!

By **Steve Korté**

Illustrated by **Lee Ferguson**

HARPER FESTIVAL

An Imprint of HarperCollinsPublishers

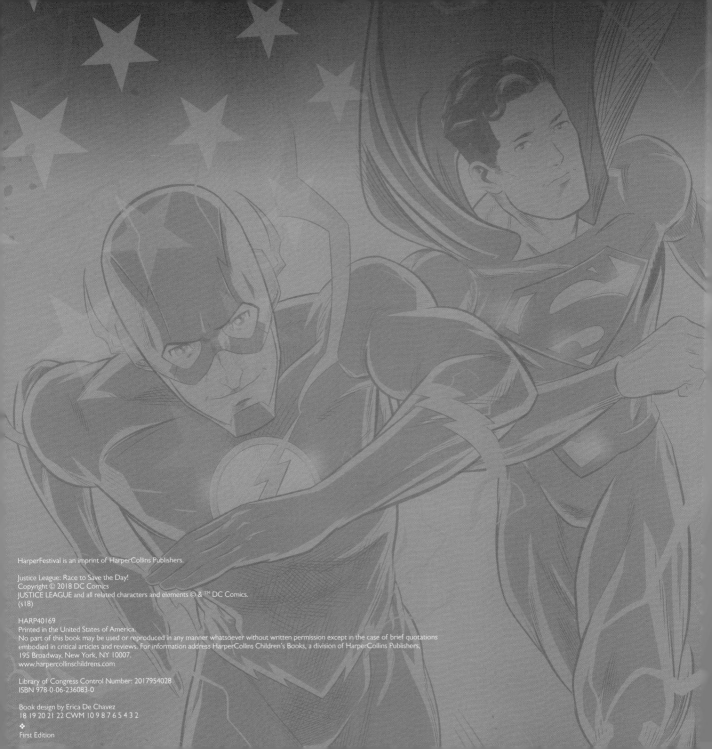

HarperFestival is an imprint of HarperCollins Publishers.

Justice League: Race to Save the Day!
Copyright © 2018 DC Comics.
JUSTICE LEAGUE and all related characters and elements © & ™ DC Comics.
(s18)

HARP40169
Printed in the United States of America.

Library of Congress Control Number: 2017954028
ISBN 978-0-06-236083-0

Book design by Erica De Chavez
18 19 20 21 22 CWM 10 9 8 7 6 5 4 3 2
❖
First Edition

The Flash and Superman stand in the park surrounded by kids. They sign autographs and take pictures with their fans. The two super heroes are going to race each other around the world. Everyone wants to be part of the big race.

The Flash is the Fastest Man Alive. He thinks he will beat the Man of Steel easily. But he runs circles around his fans to practice before the race.

Superman has super-speed. He has many other superpowers as well.
Instead of warming up for the race, he shows his fans how it feels to fly.
With two great heroes competing, no one knows who will win the race!

Not everyone in Metropolis joins in the celebration. Lex Luthor has another plan. While the super heroes are racing, he's going to rob the Metropolis Museum.

"And just in case those speed fiends are faster than they think, I've asked some friends to help slow them down," he says with a laugh.

The race begins! The Flash and Superman leave the park
amid cheers and celebration. Soon they reach the ocean.

The Flash is so fast that he runs on *top* of the water! "The surfers will like these waves," he says, as he churns up the water.

Superman leaves The Flash to make waves while he dips below the surface. He holds his breath and runs along the ocean floor!

Up ahead, Black Manta crashes into a boat. The passengers are sent tumbling into the ocean.

The Flash watches the collision, and prepares to make a quick stop to help.

But before he gets there, Aquaman swims into action! He
rescues the passengers and lifts them safely back into their boat.

Black Manta is not happy.
But the race around the world continues.

The heroes arrive in Italy.
The villain Bizarro is trying to knock over the Leaning Tower of Pisa.
Superman takes a deep breath. He'll stop Bizarro with his freeze breath!

Suddenly, Green Lantern swoops in front of the heroes. A giant green hand shoots out from his ring and grabs the villain.

"Thanks, Green Lantern!" the heroes call out.
Bizarro is angry.
But the race around the world continues.

The heroes arrive in China. They'll race along the Great Wall before crossing the Pacific Ocean and returning to Metropolis.

But they see the Joker is on the Great Wall. He pours sticky goo all over.

The Flash and Superman speed up to stop the villain.

A group of tourists are trapped in the goo!
The people who come to help them get stuck, too.

Cyborg flies into action. He melts the goo and grabs the Joker.

The heroes wave as they race by the tourists.

The Flash and Superman approach the finish line in Metropolis. It looks like it will be a tie until . . .

The Flash wins the race! He is one second faster than Superman!

Before the Man of Steel can congratulate The Flash, he pauses. "I hear an alarm at the Metropolis Museum," says Superman.

The Flash and Superman rush to the museum. They burst through the doors and find Lex Luthor holding the rare diamond on display.

The Flash races around Lex Luthor's men and ties them up. Superman deals with Lex himself.

"Are you ready to race, Luthor?" asks The Flash.
"Let's see how fast we can get you and your gang to jail!"
With a little teamwork, the Justice League is always
quick to save the day.